A Visit to
MEXICO

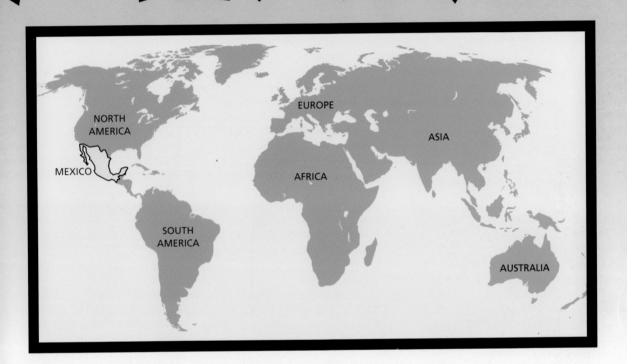

Rob Alcraft

Heinemann Library
Des Plaines, Illinois

© 1999 Reed Educational & Professional Publishing
Published by Heinemann Library,
an imprint of Reed Educational & Professional Publishing,
1350 East Touhy Avenue, Suite 240 West
Des Plaines, IL 60018

Designed by AMR
Illustrations by Art Construction
Printed and bound in Hong Kong/China by South China Printing Co.

03 02 01 00 99
10 9 8 7 6 5 4 3 2 1

Library of Congress Cataloging-in-Publication Data

Alcraft, Rob, 1966
    Mexico / Rob Alcraft.
       p. cm. — (A visit to)
    Includes bibliographical references and index.
    Summary: Introduces the land, landmarks, homes, food, clothes,
work, transport, language, schools, and recreations of Mexico.
    ISBN 1-57572-848-6 (lib.bdg.)
    1. Mexico—Juvenile literature. [1. Mexico.] I. Title.
II. Series.
F1208.5.A53 1999
972—dc21

98-37737
CIP
AC

Acknowledgments

The Publishers would like to thank the following for permission to reproduce photographs:
Colorific: pp. 5, 13; Hutchinson Library: p. 18, Edward Parker p. 7, Liba Taylor p. 16; Link: Lourdes Grobet pp. 15, 27, Philip Schedler p. 28; Panos Pictures: Paul Smith p. 8, Sean Sprague pp. 10, 17, 22, 25, 26, Liba Taylor pp. 12, 23; Reportage: Julio Etchart pp. 19, 29; Robert Harding Picture Library: Robert Francis p. 14, Robert Frerck p. 20; Still Pictures p. 11; Telegraph Color Library p. 6; Tony Stone Images: Demetrio Carrasco p. 21; Trip: Ask Images p. 9, H Sayer p. 24.

Cover photograph reproduced with permission of Kodak/Robert Harding Picture Library.

Every effort has been made to contact copyright holders of any material reproduced in this book. Any omissions will be rectified in subsequent printings if notice is given to the Publisher.

Any words appearing in bold, **like this**, are explained in the Glossary.

Contents

Mexico

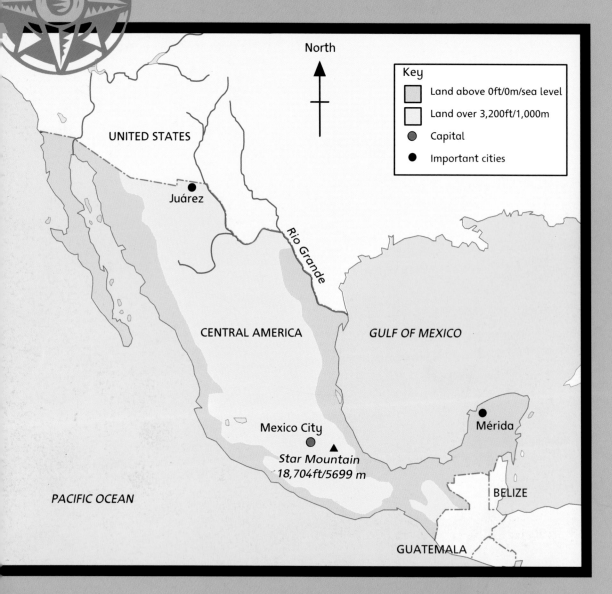

North

Key
- Land above 0ft/0m/sea level
- Land over 3,200ft/1,000m
- ● Capital
- ● Important cities

UNITED STATES

Juárez

Rio Grande

CENTRAL AMERICA

GULF OF MEXICO

Mexico City

Star Mountain
18,704ft/5699 m

Mérida

PACIFIC OCEAN

BELIZE

GUATEMALA

Mexico is in **Central America**. It shares a **border** with the United States.

Most Mexicans live in the warm, green **highlands**. They go to school and enjoy sports like you. Mexican life is also **unique**.

Land

Mexico has hot, rocky deserts. Almost half of Mexico is desert. Mexico also has grassy **plains**, forests, and long beaches.

It can be cold high up in Mexico's many mountains. There is always snow on the top of Star Mountain. It is Mexico's highest mountain.

Landmarks

The **capital** is Mexico City. 19 million people live in this big, busy city. This is twice as many people as live in New York City.

There have been cities in Mexico for thousands of years. There is a very old **temple** at Palenque (Pal-EN-kay). It was once part of a great city built by **native Indian** people called the **Mayans**.

Homes

Most Mexican homes are small. They have two or three rooms for a large family. Grandparents, uncles, and aunts often live nearby.

Homes in the country are like small farms.
The whole family joins in the work. They
grow corn and beans to eat.

Food

Meals are a time for the family to get together. Many people in Mexico like their food hot and spicy.

Tortillas are eaten with the meal.
Guacamole (Gwok-a-mol-ee) might be
served, too. It is avocadoes mashed up
with tomatoes and spices.

Clothes

Mexicans wear clothes you would recognize. They wear jeans and baseball caps or cowboy hats. Children wear uniforms to school.

In the country, many Mexicans wear **native Indian** clothing. The clothes are handmade and very colorful. Each part of Mexico has its own kind of native clothing.

Work

Mexican workers make cars, machinery, and clothes. Other workers have jobs taking care of **tourists**. They work in hotels and restaurants.

Much of the farmwork is done by hand,
or horses are used.

Transportation

Buses are the way most people travel around Mexico. The buses can get very full as everyone piles their luggage on the roof and between the seats.

People use horses and donkeys to carry things along small roads. Trucks and cars carry people and loads on big roads.

Language

Mexico was once ruled by Spain, so most Mexican people speak Spanish.

Many Mexicans speak **native Indian**
languages as well as Spanish. There are
more than 50 different native Indian
languages spoken in Mexico.

All children in Mexico go to elementary school from ages 6 to 12. After elementary school, some young people leave school to help their parents on the farm.

Mexican children study Spanish and
math. Country schools have vegetable
gardens where children also learn
about farming.

Free Time

Mexicans enjoy soccer and basketball. Many enjoy **bullfights,** too. These sports are played everywhere. Big crowds come to watch.

Many Mexican children help with the housework in their free time. They might look after the animals, too. It is work, but it can also be fun.

Celebrations

Every town and village in Mexico has its own **festival**. A band leads a parade around the streets. Everyone dresses up. There is a party and dancing.

The Day of the Dead is the time when Mexicans remember people who have died. Families take presents to the graves of their **relatives**.

The Arts

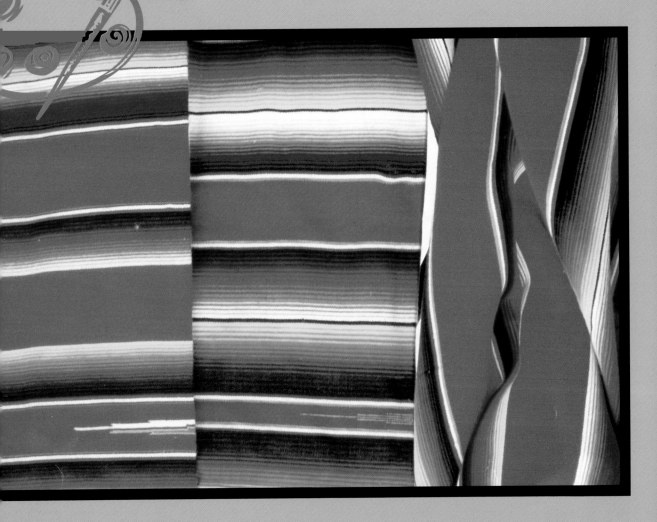

Much of the art in Mexico is made to be used as well as looked at. People make pots and weave cloth. They use colorful patterns that are very, very old.

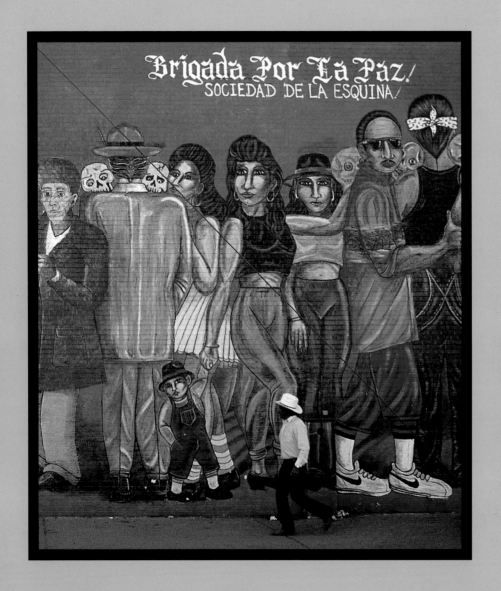

Mexican painters are famous for their wall paintings called murals. This is a mural on a building in northern Mexico.

Fact File

Name	The full name of Mexico is United Mexican States.
Capital	The **capital** city is Mexico City.
Language	Most Mexicans speak Spanish.
Population	About 90 million people live in Mexico.
Money	Mexican money is called pesos.
Religion	Most Mexicans are Catholics.
Products	Mexico produces coffee, cotton, silver, oil and gas, cars, canned food, and cloth.

Words You Can Learn

hola (o-la)	hello
adiós (adios)	goodbye
gracias (gras-e-as)	thank you
sí (see)	yes
no	no
uno (oo-no)	one
dos (doss)	two
tres	three

Glossary

border	place where two edges meet
bullfight	a sport in which a man called a matador uses a sword to fight a bull
capital	an important city where the government has its headquarters
Central America	the land between Mexico and Panama
festival	a party in which a whole town or country joins in
highlands	land where there are mountains
Mayans	people who have lived in **Central America** and Southern Mexico for more than 1,000 years
native indians	the people who first lived in Mexico before the Spanish came to rule their country
plains	flat land often covered in grass and shrubs
relative	a member of a family, for example a grandparent or a cousin
temple	a special place used for worship, like a church or mosque
tourist	a person who is traveling for pleasure
unique	different in a special way

Index

More Books to Read

Conlon, Laura. *Mexico: The Geography*. Vero Beach, FL: Rourke Book Company, Inc. 1994.

Conlon, Laura .*Visiting Mexico*. Vero Beach, FL: Rourke Book Company, Inc. 1994.

Heinrichs, Ann. *Mexico*. Danbury, CT: Children's Press. 1997.

Stein, R. Conrad. *Mexico*. Danbury, CT: Children's Press. 1995.